S0-AYQ-286

8982 HC

Fitchett, Gordon

E
Sco
FIT   Cinderella

DATE DUE	BORROWER'S NAME	NUMBER
Ap 1 0 3	Rachael	2
Ap 29 0 3	Nick	1
Ja 27 0 4	Paola	1

8982 HC

Fitchett, Gordon

E
Sco
FIT   Cinderella

MAR 2 0 2003
16.99

Cinderella

First published in the United States 2001
by Phyllis Fogelman Books
An imprint of Penguin Putnam Books for Young Readers
345 Hudson Street
New York, New York 10014

Originally published in Australia as *Cinderella*
by Clare Scott-Mitchell and illustrated by Gordon Fitchett
Text copyright © 2000 by Clare Scott-Mitchell
Pictures copyright © 2000 by Gordon Fitchett

This edition published by arrangement with Random House Australia
through International Horizons Pty Ltd
All rights reserved
Printed in Hong Kong

1 3 5 7 9 10 8 6 4 2

Library of Congress Cataloging-in-Publication Data
available upon request

The art for this book was prepared by using colored pencils.

Cinderella

Story retold by Clare Scott-Mitchell
Pictures by Gordon Fitchett

PHYLLIS FOGELMAN BOOKS  NEW YORK

Once there was a girl who was as kind as she was beautiful. Her mother had died, and her stepmother, who had two daughters of her own, hated the girl.

Cinderella was the girl's name, because her stepmother made her scrub the floors, and clean the fireplaces, and do all the heavy work, so that her clothes looked like rags. They were covered in soot and ashes and cinders from the fires, and dirt from the floors.

But the sisters never had to work at all.
They wore new clothes, and walked up and down in
front of the mirror admiring themselves and making
fun of Cinderella.

One day the King's son decided to hold a ball.
He sent invitations to the most elegant people in the land.
Cinderella's two stepsisters were invited, but not Cinderella.

How they laughed at her!
How they preened and posed and paraded up and down.
How sad and ashamed Cinderella felt.

For many days the sisters talked and fussed
and argued about what they should wear to the ball.
They asked Cinderella to help them.
"Shall I wear the red dress or the blue dress?" asked one.
"Shall I wear yellow or purple?" asked the other.

When the day of the ball arrived, Cinderella combed their hair; she buttoned their dresses and applied their makeup.
When at last they left, Cinderella sat by the fireplace among the cinders and cried. "Oh, how I wish that I could go to the ball— how I wish that I could see the Prince," she sobbed.

Suddenly a voice called, "Cinderella . . . what is the matter?
Why are you crying?"
Cinderella looked up. In front of her stood her Fairy Godmother.
"Oh!" cried Cinderella. "I wish I could go to the ball; I wish I could
see the Prince, and the King and Queen."

"Dry your eyes," said the Fairy Godmother. "You *shall* go to the ball. Go out into the garden and bring me the biggest pumpkin you can find."
When Cinderella had carried the pumpkin inside, her Fairy Godmother touched it with her wand and turned it into . . .

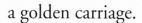

a golden carriage.

"We'll need some horses," said the Fairy Godmother.
"See if there is anything in the mouse trap."
Cinderella went to the pantry, and in the trap were
six little gray mice.
The Fairy Godmother picked up her wand.
As she touched each mouse, it turned into a fine, dappled
gray horse.
"What about a coachman?" asked Cinderella.
"Perhaps there will be a rat in the rat trap," said the
Fairy Godmother.

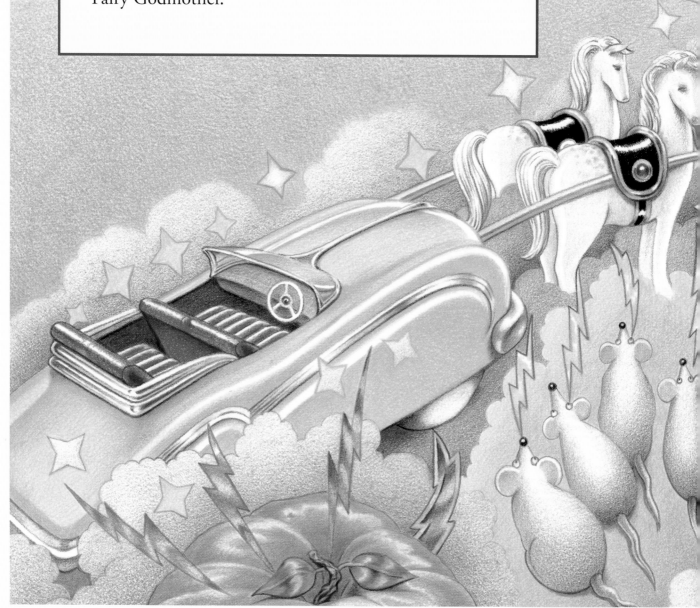

Cinderella went to look and, sure enough, there
was a fat one. As the Fairy Godmother touched it
with her wand, it turned into a splendid
coachman.

"And now for the footmen," she said.

"Cinderella, see what you can find in the cracks
between the steps."

Cinderella went to look. She found six lizards and
brought them inside.

The Fairy Godmother turned them into six
elegant footmen, who stood at attention waiting
for the carriage to move.

Then the Fairy Godmother touched Cinderella with her wand.
Her ragged clothes vanished; she was clean and shiny.
Cinderella stood in a dress of gold and silver cloth trimmed with pearls.
On her tiny feet was a pair of sparkling glass slippers, the smallest in
the world.

"Off you go now," said the Fairy Godmother. "Go to the ball, but you must be home before the clock strikes twelve. If you are late, the carriage will turn back into a pumpkin, the horses into mice, the coachman into a rat, the footmen into lizards, and your fine clothes will become rags again." "I promise to be back before twelve o'clock," said Cinderella as she stepped into the carriage.

When she reached the palace,
Cinderella stepped down from the carriage and was taken into
the ballroom to meet the King and Queen. Beside them was the Prince.
As soon as the Prince saw Cinderella, his eyes lit up like candles; he thought
that he had never seen so lovely a creature.
The Prince danced with Cinderella until the clock struck eleven.
Then supper was brought in.

Later, when the sisters came home, they called to Cinderella.
"You should have seen the beautiful lady who was at the ball."
"I wish I had been there," replied Cinderella. "Please take me with you tomorrow evening."
But the sisters only laughed and said, "Take *you*! With your rags? Not likely."

The next evening, after the sisters had left for the ball, Cinderella was sitting in the kitchen when the Fairy Godmother appeared again. She touched Cinderella with her wand, and this time her clothes were even more beautiful than the night before.

The Prince was waiting to greet her when she reached the palace.
He took her hand and led her to the place of honor.
He danced with no one but her. The supper was much later than it had
been the night before. Just as she lifted her cup to her lips, the clock
began to strike twelve.

Cinderella jumped up and ran
out of the palace as fast as she could.
As she ran down the stairs, she
tripped, and one of her little glass
slippers came off.

She did not have time to pick it up.

Quickly she stepped out of the other slipper and put it in her pocket.
Her fine clothes turned to rags and the carriage became just a pumpkin again.

The Prince was very distressed to find that his lovely Princess had disappeared. No one had seen her leave; all they had seen was a girl dressed in rags running through the palace gates. When the sisters came home, Cinderella asked them if they had seen the Princess again.

"Oh, yes," they said. "She looked even lovelier than last night. But the Prince was sad because she left in such a hurry. She dropped one of her glass slippers on the steps as she ran. He picked it up and he says that he will find her, no matter where she is."

The Prince sent messengers throughout the land, but no one could find the Princess who had been at the ball.

Then he said, "Sound the trumpets and let everyone listen: I will marry the lady whose foot fits the little glass slipper that the Princess dropped on the stairs."

So a messenger took the slipper from house to house.

All the Princesses in the land tried it on. Then all the Duchesses, then all the Grand Ladies, but it did not fit any of them.

At last the glass slipper came to the house where Cinderella lived.
Each of the two sisters tried it on, but it would not fit either of them.

Cinderella, who had been hiding behind a
curtain watching, came out and whispered,
"May I try it on?"
"You?" laughed the sisters. "A little cindermaid
like you try on the slipper?"
But the messenger said, "The Prince wants
every maiden in the kingdom to try the
slipper on."

Cinderella sat on a stool. The messenger knelt
in front of her and put the slipper on her foot.
It fit perfectly.
Then Cinderella took the matching slipper
from her pocket and put it on the other foot.

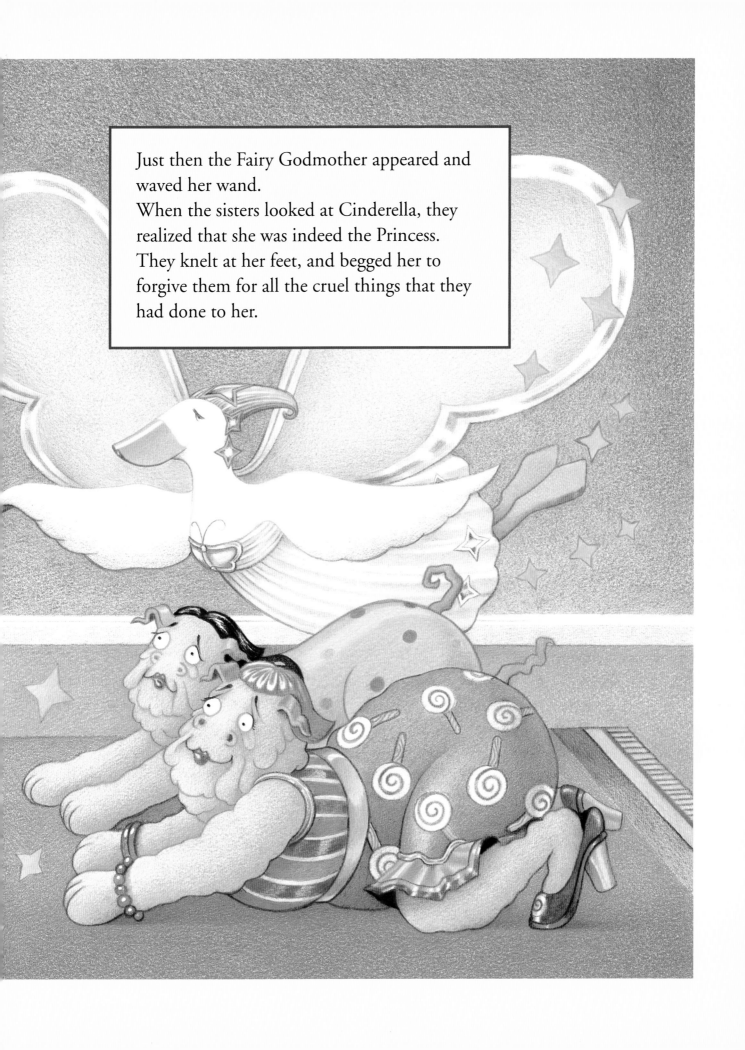

Just then the Fairy Godmother appeared and waved her wand.
When the sisters looked at Cinderella, they realized that she was indeed the Princess. They knelt at her feet, and begged her to forgive them for all the cruel things that they had done to her.

Many people came to see the wedding
of Cinderella and the Prince.
Cinderella forgave her sisters, and gave
them each a house near
the palace.
They all lived happily
ever after.